Buddy Cop 2

Written by
Hannah Bos & Paul Thureen

Developed by Oliver Butler

A SAMUEL FRENCH ACTING EDITION

SAMUEL FRENCH

FOUNDED 1830

NEW YORK HOLLYWOOD LONDON TORONTO

SAMUELFRENCH.COM

MUSIC USE NOTE

IMPORTANT BILLING AND CREDIT REQUIREMENTS

All producers of *BUDDY COP 2 must* give credit to the Authors of the Play in all programs distributed in connection with performances of the Play, and in all instances in which the title of the Play appears for the purposes of advertising, publicizing or otherwise exploiting the Play and/or a production. The name of the Authors *must* appear on a separate line on which no other name appears, immediately following the title and *must* appear in size of type not less than fifty percent of the size of the title type.

In addition the following credit *must* be given in all programs and publicity information distributed in association with this piece:

The development of *Buddy Cop 2* was made possible in part by grants from The Greenwall Foundation, The Mancini Foundation and public funds from the Fund for Creative Communities, supported by the New York State Council on the Arts and administered by the Lower Manhattan Cultural Council.

Production design support for the premiere production was provided by The Edith Lutyens and Norman Bel Geddes Foundation.

***Buddy Cop 2* was originally created and performed by The Debate Society. The play was produced in association with the Ontological Hysteric Incubator at the Ontological Theater at Saint Mark's Church in New York City, Spring 2010**

BUDDY COP 2 was originally produced by The Debate Society in association with the Ontological-Hysteric Incubator at the Ontological Theater at Saint Mark's Church, and opened on May 20, 2010. The performance was directed by Oliver Butler, with sets by Laura Jellinek, lighting by Mike Riggs, costumes by Sydney Maresca, and sound by Nathan Leigh. The production stage manager was Amy Ehrenberg, and assistant stage manager was Shelley Miles. The cast was as follows:

DARLENE NOVAK. . . . . Hannah Bos

TERRY OLSEN . . . . Paul Thureen

DON McMURCHIE . . . . Michael Cyril Creighton

BRANDI, SKYLAR . . . . Monique Vukovic

RADIO ANNOUNCER. . . . . Evan Thompson

CHARACTERS

DARLENE NOVAK – Female Police Officer (late 20's to early 30's)

TERRY OLSEN – Male Police Officer (mid to late 30's)

DON McMURCHIE – Male Police Officer (40-ish)

SKYLAR – Very frail 12 year-old girl

BRANDI – 13 year-old girl. Governor's daughter

NOTE: **BRANDI** and **SKYLAR** are to be played by the same actress. May be played by either an adult or a child.

SETTING

The small town of Shandon, Indiana.

TIME

1982

A NOTE ABOUT THE SET

Buddy Cop 2 takes place in a local small-town recreation center, where a police station has been relocated temporarily after a recent flood that destroyed the original one. The main space (the police station office) should feel added; plopped down on a basketball court (basketball court lines still visible on the floor of the office, temporary walls, etc.). The office is decorated for Christmas. A table in the office is covered with goodies and gifts that the citizens of Shandon have been dropping off at the police station.

The upstage portion of the set is a racquetball court with a plexi-glass wall or windows so people in the court can see into the main police office (downstage) and vice-versa. In the New York premiere, there was a hallway that separated the office and court. At either end of the hallway were the (unseen) door to the Chief's office and the (unseen) door to the outside.

The characters of Brandi and Skylar appear framed in sections of the existing set, maybe office windows in the police station, or in the hallway between the racquetball court and the office, or in their own separate spaces. It is important to treat the Brandi and Skylar sections in their own magical style, maybe like a children's book or a Christmas fable.

Specific stage directions in the script are written for the stage layout of the original production, but certainly other layouts would work.

SPECIAL THANKS

Shannon Sindelar, Ontological-Hysteric Incubator, East Grand Forks Police Department, Greg Widseth, Sgt. Bill Solem, Sgt. Chris Olson, Sgt. Michelle Manias, Fred Spencer, Mary Lynne Elliott, Robert Creighton, Gordon and Faythe Thureen, University of North Dakota Department of Theater Arts, Kathleen McLennan, Charlene Bos, Maggie Buchwald, Katja David Fox, Casimir Nozkowski, Ian Savage, Alice Reagan, Anne Harris, Isaac Butler, Chris Mancini, Cynthia Flowers, Marisa Savic, Alex Young, Hanna Cheek, Brian Coleman, Joel Howell, Sarah Tundermann, Anna Elliott, Jack and Judy Riggs, and Jason Black.

Preshow

(Christmas music. Wrapping paper curtain covers the stage. Racquetball can be heard being played behind it.)

Prelude: Skylar's Diary

SKYLAR. *(voice over, quietly)* The things I want with me:
My new Walkman
All my books
My smeller
My football jersey from the real football player
My pewter box with the little key
My afghan from Grandma Nelson
Panther & Wrigley
Mom
Christmas

Scene One: Police Station

(Stage is unwrapped, revealing police station office. **DON** *sits at his desk.* **TERRY** *and* **DARLENE** *are playing racquetball in the court.)*

DON. Darlene!

*(**DARLENE** leaves court and pops into the office.* **TERRY** *continues playing.)*

DARLENE. Yeah.

DON. Mary saw a garnet necklace.

DARLENE. Uh-huh.

DON. A broach actually that can be worn as a pin or hang from a chain.

DARLENE. Uh-huh.

DON. Well, they have two different lengths of chains. Opera and Princess.

DARLENE. Yeah.

DON. So one is about sixteen inches and the other is about thirty inches.

DARLENE. Uh-huh.

DON. Which one is more in style?

DARLENE. Oh, uh, I guess the Opera's more in style this season.

DON. Great, thanks.

DARLENE. Sure thing.

(Scene freezes.)

(V.O.) After everything that'd happened in Moline, I packed up and decided to take that job in tiny little Shandon. I had arrived on the 12th and we were now in the thick of the festivities.

(Scene resumes. **DARLENE** *hustles back into the court.)*

All of this happened seven years ago in the early 1980s. Two years after the flood.

*(**TERRY** serves the ball. Lights fade to black.)*

Scene Two: Brandi

*(Silhouetted in the hallway, **BRANDI** sits on a horse. Audience sees her through the stage right office window.)*

BRANDI. Skylar is a really special girl. I feel really connected to her. Did you know that we have practically the same birthday? She's the 4th, I'm the 5th. Not many people know that, I don't think I have told anyone that.

Different years though…I'm older by a year. Actually I just realized that if I went to public school we would be in the same classes sometimes. You know how they combine two years…they do that right? I'm sure we would have been really good friends. I read that she likes *Twin Sister Ranch* books which I adore. So I sent her some of those. Some of them were signed by Christine Robinson herself. My mother knows someone who knows her.

And no, Vicki Jo is not based on me. Even though I do ride a horse and my father is in politics. And I do still play the clarinet. People ask me that all the time. Oh, Skylar played the clarinet I think for a year in school too. And we both hated it. Luckily her mom was cool enough to let her quit. My parents have not been that understanding. I have a recital actually this evening at the 1st Presbyterian Church. My mother wanted me to mention that.

I'm gonna dedicate my song to Skylar. Not the classical one but we get to choose a contemporary one at the end…and mine is for her.

Scene Three: Police Station

(DARLENE and TERRY continue their game of racquet-ball. TERRY gives DARLENE instructions on how to play the game. Door buzzes.)

DON. Don't worry, I got it.

(DON exits. He returns with a plate of sweets.)

TERRY. *(through the racquetball court plexiglass)* Don, what'd we get?

DON. Fresh fudge.

DARLENE. Nice.

TERRY. Don't eat it all!

(DON sits at his desk.)

(More playing. Phone rings.)

DON. PD. Don speaking…Thank you, Merry Christmas. What can I do for you?…Yep, tickets are still available and you can get them at the rink, all proceeds go to Skylar…Ok. You too. *(hangs up)*

TERRY. *(yelling to be heard through the glass)* What time you got?

(DON doesn't hear.)

Don! What time is it?

DON. *(yelling)* 5:25.

TERRY. Ok.

(TERRY returns to playing. Phone rings again.)

DON. PD…Hi, honey…In just a few…Ok…Sure, from Patti's or the regular grocery store…Ok. How many?… Really?…Ok. Just that seems like a lot…No. I'm not. It's no problem sweetheart.

(The other line starts to ring.)

Mary, I have the other line to pick up…yep.

(He switches over to the other line.)

DON. *(cont.)* Police station…Hello, Mr. Honek…listen, Mr. Honek…Mr. Honek…Mr. Honek you're going to have to hold on just a second…hold on just a second.

(switches back to the other line)

Gotta take this, honey…yep, got it…Love you too.

*(**DON** hangs up. **TERRY** leaves the court and enters office, mopping his face with a sweat towel.)*

TERRY. Hey, Don, when you pick up that case of Buckhorn's?

DON. Oh…couple days ago. Two outta state kids had it, wrote 'em up for dope and open container.

TERRY. I'll trade you for that case of Stroh's I got.

DON. I'll go half and half.

TERRY. Alright.

*(**DARLENE** starts running back and forth in the court. **DON** notices.)*

DON. What's she doing?

TERRY. Training for her physical ability test.

(They watch her as she runs for a while. She abruptly stops and then looks back in through the window at them.)

DARLENE. Don, you heading out?

*(**TERRY** and **DON** quickly go back to their work as if they weren't watching her.)*

DON. *(loudly)* Yep.

*(**DARLENE** stretches in the court.)*

TERRY. What are you doing tonight?

DON. Making fucking cookies.

TERRY. Yeah?

DON. Charlie's school has a cookie exchange tomorrow that turns into a bake sale.

TERRY. How does that work?

DON. *(thinking)* Pretty much…I make cookies all night. Bring them in. And then I buy them back. *(shrugs)* Hey, try to get a patrol in if you can.

TERRY. Sure sure.

DON. The Chief's gonna check the log book in the cruiser. Guaranteed.

TERRY. I know.

DON. Oh…*(moving stack of files over to* **TERRY**'s *side of the desk)* I'm finished up to here.

TERRY. Got it.

DON. *(at door)* Oh, and Mr. Honek's on line 2.

TERRY. You're a son of a bitch, Don.

DON. Merry Christmas.

TERRY. Hi to Charlie and Mary.

> *(***DON** *walks out of door.* **DARLENE** *is in the court checking her heart rate,* **DON** *knocks on the glass as he passes.)*

DON. Night, sweetheart.

DARLENE. Night, Don.

> *(***DON** *pops back. Sticks head in the court.)*

DON. Hey –

DARLENE. *(startled)* Ah!

DON. Oh, sorry.

DARLENE. No, it's ok.

DON. I took a message down for you. Carol something. I put it on the board.

DARLENE. Thanks, Don.

DON. Night.

DARLENE. Night.

> *(***DON** *leaves.* **DARLENE** *exits, turning off the court lights.)*

DARLENE. I'm going to get some water.

TERRY. Ok.

> *(***DARLENE** *disappears down hallway out of view.* **TERRY** *sits at his desk and looks at the stack of files. He gets a good idea. He writes a note, clips it to the stack of files and puts it on* **DARLENE**'s *desk.* **TERRY** *goes to the food table, picks out a treat and puts it on his desk. Sits back at his desk, takes a bite of the treat. Picks up the phone.)*

TERRY. Hello, Mr. Honek...Don left. What's the problem today?...Mm-hm...Uh-huh...Mr. Honek...Mr. Honek...Mr. Honek, listen, all I can do is what you can do, and that's go over there yourself and ask them, as a courtesy, to unplug some of the lights or turn them off at a certain hour, but that's...No, because we have nothing on the books about that...

(door buzz)

DARLENE. Got it!

*(**DARLENE** crosses through the hallway, and exits to get the front door.)*

TERRY. ...I understand that, all I can tell you is you can go to the next council meeting, and try to get a, whadaya call it, a new ordinance and – ...Well great, good luck to...Wonderful Mr. Honek. We'll talk to you soon I'm sure, Merry Christmas...Say again?...Well, I don't know, I personally think it's very nice and there's a lot of people here who'd agree with me...Uh-huh...Have a good night, sir. *(hangs up)* Christ.

*(**DARLENE** has entered with a beautifully wrapped plate of treats. She adds it to the treat table. She sits at her desk.)*

DARLENE. *(looking at the files and reading the note)* Do you know what these are?

TERRY. *(looking up)* – Hm?

DARLENE. Don says I should do these. Do you know what they are?

TERRY. Oh, those are our old c-1-79 forms. I can show you how to do them.

DARLENE. That would be great, thanks.

*(**DARLENE** crosses to **TERRY**'s desk and hands him the stack.)*

TERRY. Ok, so we used to just have numbers for case numbers.

DARLENE. Yeah, Don was saying.

TERRY. So now you have to go through these and add the case type letter to it. So just give it a quick look to figure out what it is *(reading through to himself)* ...So this is an F for Domestic, so put an F in front of the existing case number, right? *(demonstrates)*

DARLENE. Right, ok.

TERRY. Put a dash in between like this...

DARLENE. Mm-hm.

TERRY. ...and then put them together, F's together, B's together, D's together, pop them over here...and when you're done with all that *(handing the files back to her)* then you're gonna file them in the box room.

DARLENE. Back by the Chief's office.

TERRY. No, those are all the water damaged files. The box room. Over there *(pointing)*...have you not been in there?

DARLENE. No, I don't think so.

TERRY. I'll show you later, half is the books salvaged from the old library and then the rest is our other files.

DARLENE. Ok, got it. I have to finish up my patrol report from yesterday and then your patrol report and the little yellow papers you gave me and then I'll start on these.

TERRY. Here, let me take some.

DARLENE. Oh that's...thank you.

*(**TERRY** takes one file from the top of the stack.)*

Just one – ok.

*(**DARLENE** sits at her desk and starts working. **TERRY** finishes his file.)*

TERRY. *(remembering something)* Oh!

(He turns on the radio. Goes to the treat table.)

Hey, you know who brought the Sticky Bars?

DARLENE. Nancy from Stumpy's. The potatoes are from Hillcrest.

TERRY. Hillcreek.

DARLENE. Right, that's what I meant.

(*TERRY looks through the food gifts. A bingo theme song starts playing on the radio and* **TERRY** *excitedly rushes back to his desk. Opens his desk drawer, pulls out a stack of bingo cards and his bingo dauber.*)

RADIO ANNOUNCER. It's 5:35, so you know what that means folks.

TERRY. Yep.

RADIO ANNOUNCER. First game we're playing card number 26973. This round is blackout. First number…N-38, N-38.

(**TERRY** *doesn't have it.*)

TERRY. (*very upset*) Damn it!

DARLENE. What's that – you know the drainage thing on the side of the curb.

TERRY. Hm?

DARLENE. On a curb, the grate with the hole on the side? What's that called?

TERRY. It's a gutter.

DARLENE. I think that's the whole thing.

TERRY. Just write gutter.

(*phone rings*)

TERRY. You wanna take one?

DARLENE. Sure.

(**DARLENE** *answers phone.* **TERRY** *watches her.*)

Shandon PD, this is Officer Novak…Merry Christmas to you…Yes, I am…Two weeks…Well, thank you. What can I do for you…Well, thank you…You too. Bye. (*hangs up*) Just wanted to wish us Merry Christmas.

TERRY. You handled that well. Oh hey, you want a sucker?

DARLENE. Nah, I have my physical ability test coming up.

TERRY. That's right.

*(**TERRY** grabs a screwdriver from his desk, jogs to the door. Holds screwdriver up to show **DARLENE**.)*

TERRY. *(cont.)* Key to Chief's desk.

(He spins it in his hand, drops it, picks it up and exits down the hall toward the Chief's office. We hear him break into the desk.)

(offstage, happily) Hah-ha!

*(He returns with a lollipop and dirty magazine. He stands watching **DARLENE** work, then looks around the room.)*

Hey, you taken a look at Don and my beer can collection.

DARLENE. I saw it but I haven't really looked at it.

TERRY. We lost some of them in the flood, but it's still pretty good. They're from all over the place. It's sort of a nice history of all the assholes *(phone rings)* we've busted for open containers or underage – *(picks up phone)* Police Station…Sure thing, hold on…*(to **DARLENE**)* What time's the candlelight vigil?

DARLENE. I don't know.

TERRY. It's on the holiday schedule. By the calendar.

DARLENE. Oh. *(She gets up to look.)*

TERRY. August 23rd.

DARLENE. 8pm.

(door buzz)

Got it!

*(**DARLENE** hustles to the door.)*

TERRY. *(back on the phone)* – 8pm, ma'am.

DARLENE. *(exiting)* Oh –

TERRY. Hold on.

DARLENE. Don said candles will be provided.

*(**DARLENE** exits.)*

TERRY. And candles will be provided…Yes, ma'am…You're very welcome…Well, we just know what everyone knows, she's not doing too good…Yep, we're just praying she holds on 'til Christmas…That *would* be a miracle… Thank you, you too. Merry Christmas. *(hangs up)*

(The phone rings again.)

Police station…*(with sudden urgency)* Sir…Sir, I need you to calm down. *(Turns off radio. Grabs a pen.)* …Ok, where are you…Are they still there…Sir, sir…I know, but I need you to calm down…What's your name, sir… *(realizing what's up)* Is this Tommy…*(laughing)* Tommy, you son of a bitch! Yer a son of a bitch! Nah, I knew it was you.

(DARLENE *returns, puts a tin on the table)*

Nah, I did…Oh Novak…Yeah, she's here. She's good. *(quickest glance at her boobs)* Medium… *(chuckling)* I can't, I'm not gonna answer that right now…Probably. *(paging through magazine as he talks)* …Say again?…Nah, can't. Chief's on vacation 'til the 1st so I'm here every night…*(surprised)* You're skating for Skylar?…No, good for you buddy…Sure, sure, uh…Put me down for a nickel a lap…Hey just a second – *(away from the phone)* Hey, Novak, my buddy Tommy is skating for Skylar, you in for a nickel a lap?

DARLENE. Yeah, put me down for a nickel.

TERRY. *(back on the phone)* All right Tommy, you got 10 cents a lap from the PD…Hey, give Don a call, maybe he'll pitch in a penny *(laughs, maybe a little too hard, at his joke)* …Listen, Tommy, I should get back to it…No, no Chief's up at Gull Lake…Alright, Merry Christmas buddy, you too. *(hangs up)* Tommy's great. *(turns radio back on)* You ever been to Canada?

DARLENE. Nope.

TERRY. Where ya been?

DARLENE. Um, to DC, the capitol, and Texas for a wedding. *(Door buzzes.)* I got it.

TERRY. Don't worry, it's not always like this.

RADIO ANNOUNCER. Another number for you folks…We got yer double nickel, G-55, G-55.

TERRY. Damn it!

(**TERRY** *puts his head in his hands, then crumples his bingo card and turns off the radio.*)

DARLENE. (*yelling from offstage*) Hey, Olsen, get out here!

(**TERRY** *gets up and exits. We hear from outside a handbell choir. They play a quick number.* **TERRY** *and* **DARLENE** *clap and then return.*)

Do they always do that with the costumes and everything?

TERRY. No, I've never seen handbells here before.

DARLENE. Did you see the little one with the bell?

TERRY. Yeah. His sign said, "We love you Skylar." They're going to Skylar's house.

DARLENE. Have you met Skylar?

TERRY. No. I saw her once at the VFW with her mom. Before she got sick.

DARLENE. I'd love to meet her. What a kid.

(*The phone rings again.*)

TERRY. Police Station. Sure thing, she's right here.

(**DARLENE** *picks up the line.*)

DARLENE. Officer Novak, can I help you.

(**TERRY** *gets up and goes over to treat table again.*)

Oh, hi Mom…I don't know…I'm not gonna…You can… 'Cause…'Cause. It's either in storage or mixed up with his stuff…Mama tell Babicka that she can just embroider another one…Get her on the phone, I know she is not gonna care.

(**DARLENE** *talks and laughs in Czech with her grandma.*)

Babicko, nevadi Ti, kdyz nedostanu zpatky povlaky na polstar?

DARLENE. *(cont.)* *(back with her mom)* See, Mom, she doesn't care.

(She holds the phone away from her ear as her mother and grandma yell at each other.)

Mama, I can't go to a barbecue, you know what's going on here…I have to go I'm at work, Mom. Love you too. *(hangs up)*

TERRY. What was that, Polish?

DARLENE. Bohemian.

TERRY. Ah, Bohemian. Hey, Novak, think fast. *(throws a racquetball at her)*

DARLENE. YOU think fast, Olsen.

(She throws it back. Then she picks up a racquet.)

TERRY. You wanna –

DARLENE. Just a little back and forth.

TERRY. Yeah?

DARLENE. Come on.

TERRY. You sure?

DARLENE. Yeah, come on.

TERRY. You ready?

DARLENE. Yep.

TERRY. Here ya go.

*(**TERRY** throws the ball to her. She swings racquet back and knocks down a shelf full of trinkets, awards and Christmas candy. Stuff goes everywhere. **TERRY** starts laughing.)*

DARLENE. Oh my God, I'm so sorry, I'm so sorry, I'm so sorry.

TERRY. *(laughing)* Novak. Come on! That's why you don't play racquetball in the office.

DARLENE. *(holding up a broken trophy)* Whose is this?

TERRY. *(still laughing)* It's Don's community spirit award.

(phone rings)

DARLENE. It's missing an arm.

TERRY. Just find it and we'll glue it on.

(The phone rings again. **TERRY** *answers it.)*

Yup?…Nope, he's up in Canada. This is Officer Olsen. *(suddenly serious)* Yes, sir. *(gestures towards* **DARLENE** *to stop making noise)* Thank you sir, that's quite an honor…How many do you need? …We certainly can provide that…Yes sir. Well there's me and…O-l-s-E-n, yes…That's correct. And Don McMurchie. I can give you his home number if… May I ask why…Ok, of course…Well, there's, uh, Officer Darlene Novak…Yes, she's right here… Ok, yes…Very good…Ok. Certainly, we will be there …Thank you, sir…Goodnight.

(He hangs up.)

(astonished) The Governor is so impressed with the spirit of Shandon, he and his wife are coming to Skate4Skylar.

DARLENE. *Wow.*

TERRY. And they've asked us to be special security for their daughter.

DARLENE. Brandi?

TERRY. Yes.

*(***DARLENE***'s jaw drops.)*

(blackout)

Scene Four: Skylar

*(Silhouetted in the hallway, **SKYLAR** lies in her bed. There is an intravenous-drip attached to her. She is very, very sick. She wears a stocking cap to cover her head. Audience sees her through the stage left office window. The window into the racquetball court is now **SKYLAR**'s bedroom window. Sound of handbells drifts in from outside.)*

SKYLAR. I told my mom I had a dream where all my teeth fell out. All over the floor by my locker. I bent down to pick them up and I put them in my pocket. I was embarrassed but I didn't care. I went out to play a game of volleyball. I won. Then I got home to put my teeth under my pillow for the tooth fairy. In the middle of the night I woke up to this giant Santa hovering over me with blood all over his beard. He said he killed someone and if I wanted my money I had better tell him my name. I think he said he hit someone but I didn't know if he meant with a car or something else. I couldn't talk though, no matter how much I tried, because I didn't have any teeth.

Scene Five: Police Station

(Back at the police station, later that night [ca. 11:30 pm]. **DARLENE** *and* **TERRY** *excitedly polishing their shoes. Music plays on the radio. Door buzzes.)*

DARLENE. Got it!

*(***DARLENE*** exits.)*

RADIO ANNOUNCER. Should be getting close to some BINGO's out there. 681-4325's the number if you win. Remember folks, this jackpot is a no-split, so 1st caller takes all. And get ready for our Midnight Madness round coming up with a triple jackpot. *(***DARLENE*** returns with more treats.)* Got yer traveling number, I-27. That's I-27.

*(***TERRY*** stops and looks at his card. Returns to shining.)*

DARLENE. What's "traveling number" mean?

TERRY. Interstate 27. So: I-27.

DARLENE. Oh. Do you have it?

TERRY. Nope.

(They polish.)

TERRY. The Governor's wife came to Shandon after the flood. Chief met her.

DARLENE. Yeah, Chief showed me the pictures.

TERRY. In the hip waders?

DARLENE. Yeah, she's pretty.

TERRY. Oh yeah.

DARLENE. Are we supposed to call her First Lady or –

TERRY. Oh, we'll be briefed on all that.

DARLENE. I hope so.

TERRY. Yeah, but we don't just talk to them. It's just when we're introduced.

(phone rings)

DARLENE. Terry, I know.

TERRY. Police department...Hi, Chuck...Nope, you're in the clear again. It's going to be the same 3 blocks as the 4th of July, so Cherry and Malvern will be blocked off...Oh, I think they'll be using all the floats, but give Don a call about that. He and Mary are on the parade committee...The Springerle? Yup we got 'em, they're delicious. Appreciate it...Alright, thanks Chuck. Merry Christmas!

(He hangs up.)

DARLENE. Is Christmas always like this here?

TERRY. God, no.

DARLENE. It feels like a very Christmasy Christmas.

TERRY. Hope so. Town's spent most of the year's budget on it. We've cancelled the Thanksgiving parade, high school's called off Homecoming...

(DARLENE puts her polished shoes down, drops to the floor and starts doing push-ups.)

Not bad, Novak.

DARLENE. *(while doing push-ups)* How many did you do?

TERRY. How many can I do?

DARLENE. No, how many did you do for your test?

TERRY. Oh, my physical ability test? I don't remember.

(finishes)

DARLENE. *(catching breath)* So push-ups, sit-ups...

TERRY. Shuttle run.

DARLENE. Shuttle run. Obstacle course?

TERRY. Yep.

DARLENE. Man. *(She gets down to start another set.)*

TERRY. Hey, if someone tries to take out the Governor tomorrow, yer not gonna be able to lift up your arms to shoot 'em.

DARLENE. *(while doing push-ups)* I could shoot 'em.

TERRY. Oh yeah?

DARLENE. Yeah.

TERRY. Oh yeah, you wanna go hit?

DARLENE. *(out of breath, struggling)* Yeah.

TERRY. Yeah?

DARLENE. Yeah.

TERRY. Three points.

DARLENE. 2 out of 3 or first to 3?

TERRY. First to 3. I wanna get you good. Don can't play for shit.

DARLENE. Yeah, Don was saying he's bad.

*(**TERRY** starts to exit after **DARLENE**, comes back, turns radio up and turns it to face the court.)*

DARLENE. Come on slowpoke.

TERRY. I'm coming.

(He grabs his bingo card, starts to head to the court then comes back, grabs the tape. As he exits the office he notices a note hanging on the bulletin board.)

Oh hey, a note here for you. Carol from Sybaris.

DARLENE. That's ok, I'll call her back later.

*(**TERRY** enters the court and tapes his Bingo card to the window. **TERRY** and **DARLENE** play a point.)*

RADIO ANNOUNCER. We got a BINGO.

TERRY. Son of a bitch!

*(**TERRY** smacks the ball against the window. Special bingo song plays for bingo winner. **TERRY** stews.)*

Your serve.

*(**DARLENE** serves. Blackout.)*

Scene Six: Brandi

(**BRANDI**, *in silhouette, practices her pop song on the clarinet.*)

BRANDI. My friend Sharon got her father to send Skylar a beta max for her room. It was on her Christmas list they published in the newspaper. My mom read it to me and told me how lucky we were and she started crying in the salon. My mom never cries in public. Then all the ladies who worked there started tearing up. The lady setting my hair almost couldn't finish. She started talking about her friend's mother who just died but said this was so much worse. In the paper it said she doesn't even have a Walkman.

(Returns to playing as lights fade.)

Scene Seven: Police Station

(Smack of a ball brings up the lights.)

DARLENE. Yessss!

*(Lights up on **TERRY** and **DARLENE** arguing a point.)*

TERRY. No, no, no, it's a do over.

DARLENE. I'm not going to do over, I won.

TERRY. That was a hinder. You can't block my shot with your body. That's called a hinder and it's a do over. It actually should be my point 'cause you didn't call the hinder.

DARLENE. I don't even know what that means, you didn't teach me that.

TERRY. Your serve.

DARLENE. Fine, my serve.

(She serves. They play the point. Phone rings.)

TERRY. You're losing. You get the phone.

*(**DARLENE** exits to office. **TERRY** stays in the court and hits.)*

DARLENE. Shandon PD, can I help you this is Novak…Oh hey, Don…Terry's in the court playing with himself. *(loudly)* Terry, it's your boyfriend.

*(**DARLENE** exits to get water. **TERRY** enters office, picks up phone.)*

TERRY. Hey, Don…Yeah, Brandi's doing some kind of special performance…Yeah!…They come in around 2pm and head straight to the rink…No, they have their own escort, we're just doing some security…Hey, hey, Don, I gotta tell ya, Don, they just need me and Novak…No, they did background checks…Yeah…NO, I know…I hear ya, Don, I hear ya…I know me too…Alright… Sorry, buddy…Night.

*(**DARLENE** enters, pulls her message off the bulletin board.)*

DARLENE. You mind if I make a personal call real quick?

TERRY. Go ahead.

(**TERRY** *notices she's waiting for him to leave.*)

Oh. I'll go hit.

(**TERRY** *exits to court.* **DARLENE** *dials phone.*)

DARLENE. Hi Dennis, my name is Darlene Novak. I left a message with Carol this morning...about getting a refund for a wedding gift I got...Correct....

(**TERRY** *hears this, starts listening through the glass. He's loving it.*)

Majestic Whirlpool Suite...Uh-huh...Can you just refund them?...Well, can I get the cash value, then?... Right but I got divorced...I don't think that's really the issue here...No, but I got divorced you understand and – ...Oh my God, ok, well, then what do you get?... Jacuzzi's inside the room?...Uh, huh. Champagne toast or a whole bottle...How nice.

(*puts the phone down for a second to think*)

Christ.

(*door buzz*)

TERRY. Got it.

(**TERRY** *exits court, disappears down hallway.* **DARLENE** *picks up the phone again.*)

DARLENE. Ok great, well, how about the day after Christmas?...(*angrily*) No, no, you said I still have a month before it expires...Oh waitwaitwait. Sorry...I mean the 26th of this month...No, I know, my fault. I'm in a town called Shandon and we've got a little girl here who has cancer, so we're all coming toget– ...Yeah, you heard about it...Yeah, it's pretty incredible...I don't know, I just moved here...Is that right?...Put me down for August 26th...And it's ok if it's just me?

(**DARLENE** *laughs.* **TERRY** *enters carrying a watermelon wrapped in a Christmas bow.*)

DARLENE. *(cont.)* I'm sure it has…Thanks, Merry Christmas to you, too, Dennis. Bye. *(hangs up)*

TERRY. *(really enjoying this)* So…You making a reservation?

DARLENE. Yeah, I got a gift certificate for my wedding and it's about to expire, it's this whole ordeal…

TERRY. Yeah, Sybaris, I've seen the billboards, it's like a… adult or romantic hotel –

DARLENE. There's pools in the rooms, it's supposed to be nice, I don't know. All my cousins chipped in for it.

TERRY. Great, great. You're going Thursday?

DARLENE. Yeah.

TERRY. Great. *(whispering in a husky voice)* Sybarissssss.

DARLENE. Yup, that's the commercial they sing on T.V.

TERRY. Sybarissss.

(He laughs.)

Just joshing ya. Hey, you like swimming, you should just go down to the river.

DARLENE. Don said it's crowded this time of year.

TERRY. Yeah, that's true. Wait 'til school starts. Hey, I gotta get going. Said I'd make an appearance at the Jingle Mingle at the VFW.

DARLENE. I'm gonna stay and straighten up a bit.

TERRY. Ok, but hun, leave the shelf though. Don loves tinkering with things. He'll fix it.

DARLENE. Yeah, I know, I just wanna clean up a little bit.

TERRY. Ok. *(picking up a gift wrapped bottle from the treat table)* Hey, grab a bottle of whiskey. There's one for each of us.

DARLENE. I don't drink anymore. I just drink beer. And champagne.

TERRY. Okey-doke. *(grabbing another bottle)* Hey, big day tomorrow.

DARLENE. Yeah!

*(**TERRY** exits.)*

TERRY. Night, Novak.

DARLENE. Goodnight!

(*DARLENE takes a deep breath and puts on her lipstick. She grabs her purse and files something. She feels something in the office with her. She quickly turns off all the lights and walks briskly out of the station.*)

Scene Eight: Skylar

*(Summer night sounds in distance. **SKYLAR** lies in her bed.)*

SKYLAR. It's Christmas when the snow starts to fall the man dressed all in red says. The man in red who's in the corner. In my room most of the time, watching me. No one else sees him. My mom doesn't see him. He's there in the middle of the night whenever I wake up because I hurt. Sometimes I keep my eyes closed when I wake up so he'll think I'm still asleep. But if I peek out, he's always there smiling at me. His teeth are black which is a little scary. Sometimes he's here in the day too when mom gives me my pill or when she puts the needle in my arm and I think maybe he likes being there to watch all the medicine go from the bag into the tube and into my arm. He only talks to me when there's no one around. And he always talks about Christmas. How when the snow starts to fall he'll fly through the air in his red suit flapping his arms and come and get me. His eyes are yellow and sometimes red when it's really really dark and I bet he can see through everyone's roof and see all the kids sleeping on Christmas Eve, thinking about toys and nice things. Thinking of getting a fire truck so they can pretend to grow up to be a fireman or a toy car so they can pretend they're going to grow up to be a racecar driver. But the man in red says that kids don't always grow up. And that's the kids that he's looking for.

Scene Nine: Police Station

*(The next day. **DON** is fixing the shelf. **DARLENE** is running back and forth in the racquetball court.)*

DON. Darlene! Start a pot of coffee.

*(**DARLENE** exits court, goes down the hall.)*

DARLENE. Sanka?

DON. Decaf.

(phone rings)

PD, this is Don…Oh, thanks for calling me back…You do, wonderful, and all the stuff comes with it, beard, belt…Great, ok.

*(**TERRY** comes through the hallway with a big cardboard box, taped with duct tape, with "**BRANDI**" scrawled all over it in black marker.)*

What time do you open tomorrow?…Great. Say, I'm coming up from Shandon, will I be able to see you guys when I exit off the interstate?…Yep, that's us…Yep, Skylar…It is, actually. We have a parade tomorrow and I'm leading it as Santa, so…Oh, you don't have to do that…Well, thank you, that's very generous. We really do appreciate that…Ok…Will do…Thank you. Merry Christmas to you. *(hangs up)* Nice guy. Hey Terry, you still ok to work the double tomorrow?

TERRY. *(**TERRY** starts changing into his recently polished dress shoes.)* Oh yeah, sure thing.

DON. I'm driving up to Grafton to pick up the suit.

TERRY. That's right.

DON. What's the box?

TERRY. Someone left it out front for us to take to Brandi.

DON. No way. They won't let you in with that. The secret service guys –

TERRY. No, I know, I'll just hold onto it and figure out what to do with it later.

DON. I'm a little miffed.

TERRY. Yeah.

DON. It's bullshit. They take her over me?

TERRY. It is bullshit.

DON. Because of nothing.

TERRY. I know.

DON. And then it's *her* representing the town, when she –

TERRY. When she just got here. Yeah, I know. I know, Don. It should be you and me, but – You know it's not personal, they have their processes and –

DON. I know, I know. Thanks, Terry. It's no big deal.

(**DON** *puts something away in the desk door and slams it shut.*)

TERRY. Yeah, it's probably gonna be just a big pain in the ass anyway. Photographers and –

(**DARLENE** *enters with coffee pot.*)

DARLENE. I'm getting kind of excited!

(*pours coffee*)

Terry?

TERRY. No. So we might be stuck until they release us from the rink. You ok to stay?

DON. I just have The Muscle Tones at 9pm, so if I can make that.

TERRY. Sure.

DARLENE. What's The Muscle Tones?

DON. It's my men's vocal group.

DARLENE. No! Really?

DON. Yeah.

DARLENE. Don, you're a choir boy?

DON. (*trying to keep his cool*) We perform pops songs and originals and then do madrigals at Christmas.

TERRY. They're really good.

DON. We're singing for Skylar tonight.

DARLENE. I would love to come.

DON. You can't. It's in her house…We'll do a concert for the general public at Christmas.

DARLENE. December Christmas?

DON. Christmas Christmas. Bill Solem, the football coach, he's our lead tenor. He's out of town right now, so we can't do a full concert.

DARLENE. Too bad, I would love to hear you sing sometime.

(beat)

*(***DON*** gets up. Walks towards ***DARLENE.*** He stands in front of her desk. He sings a verse of the madrigal "Masters in This Hall" while glaring at ***DARLENE.****)*

DON. There ya go.

*(Phone rings. ***DARLENE*** quickly picks it up. ***DON*** returns to his desk.)*

DARLENE. Shandon PD this is Novak, can I help you…Oh hello…Yes he's here too…Oh, ok…Yes sir, no problem at all…Nope, no problem, we'll be right over…Sure thing, bye. *(hangs up)* The Governor arrived early, they want us at the rink right now.

TERRY. Ok, let's do it.

DARLENE. Keys?

TERRY. Yep.

DARLENE. Bye, Don.

*(***TERRY*** and ***DARLENE*** exit. ***TERRY*** pats ***DON*** on the back as he crosses. ***DON*** is left alone drinking his coffee. A tinsel decoration falls from the ceiling. ***DON*** looks up at it. Lights fade.)*

Scene Ten: Skate4Skylar

(The racquetball court has transformed into the rink. **BRANDI** *roller skates in a circle, warming up.)*

RINK ANNOUNCER. Ladies and gentleman, please leave the rink. Lap-skate will resume after the performance. And now, it is my pleasure to introduce our state's first daughter.

(Lights shift and **BRANDI** *skates her routine to "Arabian Dance" from the Nutcracker Suite. As she skates, lights raise on* **DON.** *He is sitting alone in the station, listening to the performance on the radio. Lights fade on the station as she finishes her routine. Applause.)*

*(***BRANDI***, out of breath, picks up a microphone and addresses the crowd.)*

BRANDI. Thank you very much. I'm happy I could be here today to perform my solo. Especially because I made a few mistakes when I did it on ice back home last December.

Anyways, we all know how important it is to give. Skylar and the whole town of Shandon has really taught me about the true importance of Christmas. It's not the gifts or even about getting things you want, it's about giving. Making a sacrifice. And knowing in your heart what to do.

My Grannie Jean passed away last summer from cancer and I was at sailing camp and I never got to say goodbye.

(She puts the mic down and picks up a pair of scissors. She cuts a big chunk out of her hair and holds it in the air.)

This is for Skylar and my Grannie Jean!

(She drops the hair to the ground and returns to cutting as the lights fade.)

Scene Eleven: Police Station

(*TERRY and DARLENE are wearing Skate4Skylar hats. There's also one on DON's desk.*)

TERRY. Everyone just went crazy!

DARLENE. People went nuts.

DON. Yeah, I could hear that on the radio.

TERRY. The Governor's face just… (*makes expression of face dropping*)

DARLENE. And his wife just… (*makes a face*) Right?

DON. You could see that?

TERRY. Oh yeah.

DARLENE. (*overlapping*) Oh yeah, we were right there next to them.

DON. So, they didn't know she was going to do it?

TERRY. I really don't think so the way he looked, I really don't think so.

DON. Come on.

TERRY. I really don't. You could see it on him he didn't expect it. She finished her speech. The crowd was completely quiet. And then she started cutting.

DARLENE. Cut, cut, cut, hair all over the rink.

(*phone rings*)

DON. PD, this is Don…Hey, Nelson, what's the deal…Aw, jeez…Ok…Got it…Sounds good (*looks at his watch*) see you guys there. (*hangs up*) Guess she's doing worse. We're going to have to sing outside her window.

DARLENE. You guys are great.

DON. Oh, on the radio, they said they're making Brandi's hair into a wig for Skylar.

DARLENE. Oh my God!

DON. Someone called in and said they could make it into a wig.

TERRY. How do you…

DON. I don't know.

(Pause as they contemplate the idea.)

DARLENE. Isn't that something.

DON. Did you see Skylar's mom?

TERRY. Yeah, she was sitting right next to the governor… I can't imagine what she's going through…but she looked pleased. I think all this means a whole lot to her.

DARLENE. Yeah.

DON. Yeah.

(They sit quietly.)

(looks at his watch, gets up to leave) Well, I gotta get over there. Thanks for the hat.

TERRY. Hey, time for a quick beer?

DON. No. Sure. Quick beer.

TERRY. Or we have that glug.

DON. Darlene?

DARLENE. Let's do the glug.

*(**TERRY** exits. **DARLENE** gets mugs from a shelf.)*

Don you want your penguin mug or the Christmas ones?

DON. Let's do the Christmas ones.

DARLENE. I'm sorry you couldn't be there, Don.

DON. Thanks, Novak.

*(**TERRY** enters with a jug of glug.)*

TERRY. *(trying different pronunciations)* Glug? Glug? Glug?

DARLENE. Glug.

DON. *(same way)* Glug.

TERRY. *(Pouring. Same way)* Glug.

DON. This is Chief's recipe.

DARLENE. Ooh.

TERRY. Yeah, it's this weird thing he made up based on the 12 days of Christmas.

DON. Yeah, it's 12 ounces of rum, 11 raisins, 10 somethings, 2 cans of beer…

DARLENE. There's beer in it?

DON. I think he said cognac, wine, rum and beer.

DARLENE. What's the one?

DON. One cherry I think. Right?

TERRY. I dunno.

DARLENE. It smells good.

TERRY. You're supposed to drink it hot, but I like it. Hey, *(raising his glass)* Merry Christmas guys.

DON & DARLENE. Merry Christmas.

DON. To making it two more days.

DARLENE. *(upbeat)* Hang in there, Skylar.

TERRY. To two more days.

(*They drink.* **DON** *chugs his.*)

DON. Ok, now I really got to get going.

TERRY. Go to it, Don.

DARLENE. Sing good, Don.

DON. Will do. Night, guys.

TERRY & DARLENE. Night.

(*Beat.* **TERRY** *and* **DARLENE** *sip and smile.*)

DARLENE. What a day.

TERRY. What a day.

TERRY. Wanna go hit?

DARLENE. Yeah.

(*They start to get ready.*)

I did that too, when I was little. I cut the front really short and showed my mom and she freaked out.

TERRY. *(beat)* God, that would be something to see Don sing for Skylar!

DARLENE. I know!

(*They rush towards the court.*)

Grab the glug!

TERRY. Good idea.

> (**TERRY** *grabs the glug, swigs, enters the court.* **DARLENE**
> *and* **TERRY** *play, drink and talk…*)

What are you doing later tonight?

DARLENE. Going home to sleep.

TERRY. You wanna catch one of the holiday bands? All the
good local guys come together to play.

DARLENE. Maybe. Where?

TERRY. Swanky's, Spanky's or Zingers. Depends on the
night, I can make a call. I used to play with all those
guys in high school.

DARLENE. We'll see.

TERRY. You did good tonight.

DARLENE. Thanks, you too. We did some pretty big stuff up
in Moline when I was there. There were some really
big international people that came for conferences at
the factory.

TERRY. You didn't like it there? Too big for you?

DARLENE. No, I loved it. I just had to get out. The station
was really good though.

TERRY. Things worked different over there?

DARLENE. *(laughing a little.)* Yeah!

TERRY. Didn't close at midnight?

DARLENE. Didn't close at midnight.

TERRY. More than four cops.

DARLENE. More than four cops. Didn't self-dispatch. Had
about a dozen patrol cars. A bomb squad. K-9 unit…

TERRY. Did you guys have a Varda machine?

DARLENE. Oh yeah, a couple.

TERRY. Man, I want one of those. So you left because of the
divorce?

DARLENE. Yep.

TERRY. How long were you married?

DARLENE. Three months. You guys often drink during your
shift?

TERRY. No no, just special occasions.

(The door buzzes.)

I'll get it.

DARLENE. It's too hot in here.

TERRY. Yeah, it's hot.

*(They exit the court. **TERRY** goes to the door. **DARLENE** goes into the office. **TERRY** enters with tomatoes.)*

DARLENE. Christmas tomatoes.

TERRY. Yep!

DARLENE. Can I have one?

TERRY. Sure.

(She takes one and starts to eat it like an apple.)

DARLENE. Oh, hey…what happened with Don's background check. You mind if I ask?

*(**TERRY** sits at his desk and pours more glug.)*

TERRY. It's fucking stupid. He had a warrant in Oklahoma for an outstanding traffic violation that he forgot to pay.

DARLENE. That's it?

TERRY. Yeah. That's it. And he can't get it off his record. Mine's clean and I did much worse stuff.

DARLENE. Like what?

TERRY. You know how it is. Just stupid kid stuff.

DARLENE. Like what?

TERRY. I was just a hellion when I was young. A lot of cops are like that. And Don's always been by the books. It's stupid.

DARLENE. Man.

TERRY. Your ex a cop?

DARLENE. Nope, he's not. I don't really wanna talk about it.

TERRY. Sorry. Got any pets?

*(**DARLENE** starts to cry.)*

DARLENE. I'm sorry. Give me a second. Nope. No pets. Anymore.

TERRY. Let's put on some music.

DARLENE. That'd be nice.

(**TERRY** *turns on the radio.*)

Terry?

TERRY. Yeah?

DARLENE. What's in that box?

TERRY. Uh, I don't know. Somebody left it here for Brandi.

(*They look at it, suddenly struck by how suspicious it looks.*)

DARLENE. Should we open it?

TERRY. Maybe we should.

(*They cautiously open the box, dig through a bunch of packing peanuts, and pull out a metal Christmas tree.*)

DARLENE. What is it?

TERRY. Some kind of metal Christmas tree. That's a terrible gift for a 13 year old.

DARLENE. Yeah.

TERRY. You should keep it.

DARLENE. No.

TERRY. Come on keep it. Brandi's gone, what are we gonna do with it.

DARLENE. Well, I kinda like it.

TERRY. It's a house warming gift. From me to you.

DARLENE. Thanks, Terry. That's very nice of you.

TERRY. I'm a nice guy.

DARLENE. (*noticing the song on the radio*) Oh, I just got this tape!

(**TERRY** *and* **DARLENE** *are getting a little tipsy.* **TERRY** *turns up the radio. As he does,* **DARLENE** *takes off her glasses.* **TERRY** *looks up and catches her putting on lipstick.*)

TERRY. It's weird having a girl here.

DARLENE. Yeah?

(They look at each other. Awkward. Flirty.)

TERRY. You like dancing?

DARLENE. Yeah.

TERRY. Not me.

DARLENE. Oh.

(stare at each other more)

Terry…

TERRY. Yeah?

DARLENE. Seriously…am I gonna pass my physical ability test?

TERRY. Oh yeah, don't worry about it, don't worry about it. You'll do fine.

(Realizing he needs to confess:)

TERRY. I never had the physical ability test.

DARLENE. Did Don?

TERRY. Don didn't have it either.

DARLENE. Has anyone ever done it?

TERRY. No.

*(**DARLENE** considers the situation.)*

DARLENE. I'm not supposed to know that, right?

TERRY. Nope.

(beat)

Hey, let's get outta here.

DARLENE. Yeah.

(They get ready to leave.)

TERRY. Maybe we'll go to Zingers.

DARLENE. What kind of music do they play?

TERRY. Rock and roll.

(They pass the treat table on the way to the door.)

DARLENE. I'm gonna take a cake.

TERRY. Yeah, take whatever you want.

DARLENE. I'm gonna take two.

TERRY. I'll grab your box.

> (**TERRY** *picks up the box with the tree inside. They turn off the lights and exit down the hall.*)

DARLENE. My best friend in high school was named Terry. She was a girl though.

TERRY. Alright.

> (*Lights fade.*)

Scene Twelve: Skylar

(**SKYLAR** *in her bed, VERY sick, seemingly near death. Quiet singing [Masters in This Hall] is heard outside her window.* **SKYLAR** *hears the sound of boot-steps on the roof and looks up. We see* **TERRY** *and* **DARLENE** *climb up on* **SKYLAR**'s *roof and then start throwing handfuls of packing peanuts from the metal Christmas tree box over the edge of the roof.* **SKYLAR** *has pulled herself up, using her IV stand for support, to look out her window.* **SKYLAR** *does not see packing peanuts, but "real" snow falling outside her window. She collapses.*)

Scene Thirteen: Police Station

(Next morning. A baseball game plays on the radio. Lights up on **TERRY** *playing racquetball. Phone rings.* **TERRY** *exits the court, picks up the phone.)*

TERRY. Morning, Police Department…Yes…What?…

*(***TERRY*** sits. Listening to horrible news.)*

(overlap:)

(In the stage right window, lights up on **BRANDI**, *chopped hair, playing the sad pop song on her clarinet. Clarinet image fades.)*

*(***TERRY*** hangs up. He dials the phone.)*

Novak, meet me at Skylar's house.

(Lights fade.)

Scene Fourteen: Police Station

(DARLENE sorts through the box of SKYLAR's things. Pills. IV bags. Antifreeze. A diary. TERRY stands in the racquetball court. Destroyed. He exits the court, enters office and shares a look with DARLENE.)

TERRY. So the dad's not in the picture.

DARLENE. Ok.

TERRY. We'll have to track down a number somehow, he needs to get a call.

DARLENE. What do we tell people?

TERRY. Nothing yet.

DARLENE. Well, there's supposed to be the vigil after the parade and the gift drive's still going on –

TERRY. I know, I know, we just need to wait until we deal with Skylar's mom.

DARLENE. OK.

TERRY. How ya doing, Novak?

DARLENE. I don't know.

TERRY. I told HTH we'd call when we got in.

DARLENE. Ok.

(We see SKYLAR stand up in the racquetball court and make her way, groggily, towards the police station office. She slowly struggles down the hall, unseen, over the course of Terry's phone call.)

TERRY. *(dials phone)* Greg Steiner, please…Terry Olsen…Hi Greg. Yep, we're here…Um, I really can't tell…It was her mom…She put it in the IV, I think…Yeah, Novak called poison control…Yep, we just did, that's what they said to do, too…Ok…Got it…Ok…No a neighbor got suspicious, confronted her, and she just split… How soon…Ok, thanks Greg. *(hangs up)* The helicopter's on its way. I got to get going, you ok to stay?

DARLENE. Yeah.

TERRY. Ok, you keep trying to get a hold of Don and if anyone else calls, don't say anything.

(TERRY turns, and he and DARLENE see SKYLAR standing in the doorway. This is the first time we've seen her as she actually is: tiny, scarily frail, haggard.)

SKYLAR. I'm thirsty.

(SKYLAR wobbles, TERRY catches her as she collapses. He puts her gently in the chair.)

DARLENE. Terry get her something to drink!

TERRY. We have a case of Squirt.

DARLENE. Terry, get her a Squirt.

SKYLAR. Water.

DARLENE. Terry, get her some water.

(TERRY rushes out.)

(SKYLAR's head droops.)

You want something to eat?

(SKYLAR shakes her head no. Phone rings.)

Shandon PD…What? …I don't kno – …It starts right after the parade…I don't know…There's supposed to be some reception thing at the church, I don't know, Merry Christmas. *(hangs up)*

(TERRY returns with water.)

TERRY. Here ya go.

(She takes a sip.)

They're gonna take you to a really good hospital to make sure you're ok.

(SKYLAR shivers. TERRY runs back into the court, grabs a blanket SKYLAR had been using in there, rushes back and wraps it around SKYLAR.)

SKYLAR. Where's Mom?

DARLENE. We're trying to find her.

(DARLENE walks over to the box of SKYLAR's belongings. SKYLAR watches her. Confused.)

DARLENE. I need to take a look at some of the stuff I picked up from your house, ok?

(**SKYLAR** *looks around the police station.* **DARLENE** *continues to go through her things.*)

SKYLAR. Is this a real police station?

DARLENE. Well –

TERRY. Well, it's a police station now, it wasn't before. We had the flood you know a couple years ago so we moved into the rec center. They put up these walls – (*phone rings*)

(**DARLENE** *grabs the phone.*)

DARLENE. PD…Hey, Mary…He hasn't. Ok…Yeah, yeah, well if he comes home first, just have him give me a call…No, no, just parade details…Ok, you too, Mary. Bye. (*hangs up*)

(*Door buzzes, startling everyone.*)

Got it.

(**TERRY** *exits.*)

SKYLAR. (*spotting bingo cards on* **TERRY**'s *desk*) Who plays bingo?

DARLENE. Terry. He has a gambling addiction.

SKYLAR. My mom plays bingo.

DARLENE. At the VFW?

(*shrugs.*)

What nights does she go?

(**SKYLAR** *starts to fall asleep. The shelf* **DARLENE** *broke earlier falls off the wall again.* **DARLENE** *and* **SKYLAR** *look at it.*)

Are you ok?

(**TERRY** *comes back with an amazing plate of treats and a pineapple with a bow. He looks at the collapsed shelf.* **DARLENE** *waves him down the hall and he exits towards the Chief's office.*)

SKYLAR. Is it weird carrying a gun?

DARLENE. Nope it's my job.

SKYLAR. Ever scared someone's gonna grab it from behind?

DARLENE. There's a strap on the top.

SKYLAR. But someone could pull that off quick, right?

DARLENE. Is there someone behind me, Skylar?

>   (**SKYLAR** *gets very, very quiet. She starts shivering. Silence.* **TERRY** *comes back in.*)

TERRY. Novak…I need to – … (*sweetly so as not to alarm* **SKYLAR**) can we chat out in the hall for a second.

DARLENE. You ok?

>   (**SKYLAR** *nods.*)

You sure?

>   (*She nods again.*)

TERRY. We'll be right down the hall, sweetheart.

>   (**TERRY** *and* **DARLENE** *go out into the hall to talk.*)
>
>   (**SKYLAR** *carefully gets up. Walks to the box and pulls out her diary. Sound of bells.* **SKYLAR** *freezes.* **DON** *comes down the hallway dressed as Santa, bells jingling on his shoes. He enters.* **DON** *looks at* **SKYLAR**, *confused.* **SKYLAR** *stares at* **DON**…*seeing "The Man in Red."*)

SKYLAR. I might not be sick anymore.

>   (**TERRY** *and* **DARLENE** *enter.*)

DARLENE. Don! This is Don, he's another police officer here.

>   (**DARLENE** *rushes over to help* **SKYLAR** *sit [in center chair] as* **TERRY** *goes to* **DON** *and whispers to him to catch him up.* **SKYLAR** *stares at* **DON**, *terrified.*)
>
>   (*The phone rings.*)

PD…What?…I don't know what you're talking about, ma'am…I have no idea what you're talking about… I'm sorry, I can't talk about that. I'm gonna have to go now.

>   (*Hangs up.*)

DON. Is there still a parade?

(Phone rings again.)

TERRY. PD…Ok…Ok…Call back if you see her leave *(hangs up)*. *(to* **DON***)* Neighbor saw her back at the house. Let's go.

DON. I'll stay with Skylar and wait for the chopper.

TERRY. You sure.

DON. Yep.

DARLENE. Alright, let's go.

*(***DARLENE*** and ***TERRY*** rush out. ***DON*** sits with ***SKYLAR***. Phone rings.)*

DON. PD…I'm gonna stop you right now…We're not releasing any information about that.

(He hangs up the phone. He turns on the radio. Christmas music, which is suddenly interrupted.)

RADIO ANNOUNCER. Alright folks, we're gonna take a little break from the Christmas tunes. Here's something else for you.

*(The studio version of the pop song ***BRANDI*** had played on clarinet earlier comes through the radio. The sound expands to take over the whole space, and lights shift. The song continues, and ***DON*** and ***SKYLAR*** are now flying through the air in the helicopter on the way to the hospital, looking down as they sail over the rooftops. Behind them, ***TERRY*** and ***DARLENE*** draw their guns, and in a flash of light, we see them burst through the racquetball court door [now the door to ***SKYLAR****'s mom's house]. Lights fade on the court.)*

Scene Fifteen: The Future

(**SKYLAR** *remains seated center stage in darkness.*)

DARLENE. *(V.O.)* That night was a humid but hopeful Christmas Eve for those who had yet to hear the news. By the morning of August 25th the joy of this strange holiday had dissolved into confusion, anger, and an unexpected kind of sadness. But we'd all recover.

(Behind **SKYLAR**, *in the space that was the racquetball court we see a silhouette of the future...* **TERRY**, **DARLENE** *and* **DON** *decorating a Christmas tree.*)

Skylar would be placed with a foster family in a nearby town and Shandon would soon become quiet...just like we like it. By the time the Governor made a surprise return to dedicate our brand new police station, Brandi's hair was long and beautiful again.

Terry and I would become great partners and he'd introduce me to his friend Tommy who I'd eventually start a family with. Soon, Chief would retire and Don would get promoted.

Seven years and four months later...on a *real* Christmas morning...we'd pull a frozen body out of the river. I'd wait with her until county came to take her away, looking through the bag she'd tied to her body. Soggy books and stuffed animals. Some letters and cards. Her high school diploma. An old jersey.

That afternoon, I would page through an old case file and make a phone call to a mother in prison.

I'd go to sleep that night, thinking of my own kids hugging tightly their new treasures, dreaming of what they'd grow up to be.

(Lights fade on the court area.)

Scene Sixteen: The Past

(**SKYLAR** *sits center stage. She transforms…she is now healthier, as if we're hearing a diary entry from six months before the start of the play.*)

SKYLAR. Yesterday I woke up in the car on the way back from Cincinnati. I always fall asleep on the way to my treatments but Mom says that's good because it would hurt if I was awake.

I'm kinda glad I got cancer. It's not so bad so far. I got a jersey from a real football player. I'm not a football fan but it was still cool. I like hockey.

I kinda want a Walkman.

And I had a horrible haircut before this. Mom shaved my head when I got cancer 'cause it was all going to fall out anyway. Better than the perm.

Today a psychologist came to our house to talk to me. She told me when I die I can have all the things around me that I love. That I could pick what those things were. So I'm thinking about that. Tired. More tomorrow. Good night.

(*blackout*)

End of Play

COSTUME PLOT

DARLENE
    Police Uniform
    Belt and Holster (with gun)
    Skate4Skylar Baseball Cap (added)
    Dress Shoes
    Racquetball Sneakers
    Purse

TERRY
    Police Uniform
    Belt and Holster (with gun)
    Skate4Skylar Baseball Cap (added)
    Dress Shoes
    Racquetball Sneakers

DON
    Police Uniform
    Belt and Holster (with gun)
    Skate4Skylar Baseball Cap (added)
    Santa Claus Costume (with bells)

BRANDI
    Horse-riding Outfit (with crop)
    Clarinet Recital Dress
    Ice Skating Nutcracker Costume

SKYLAR
    Nightshirt
    Woolen Hat
    Slippers

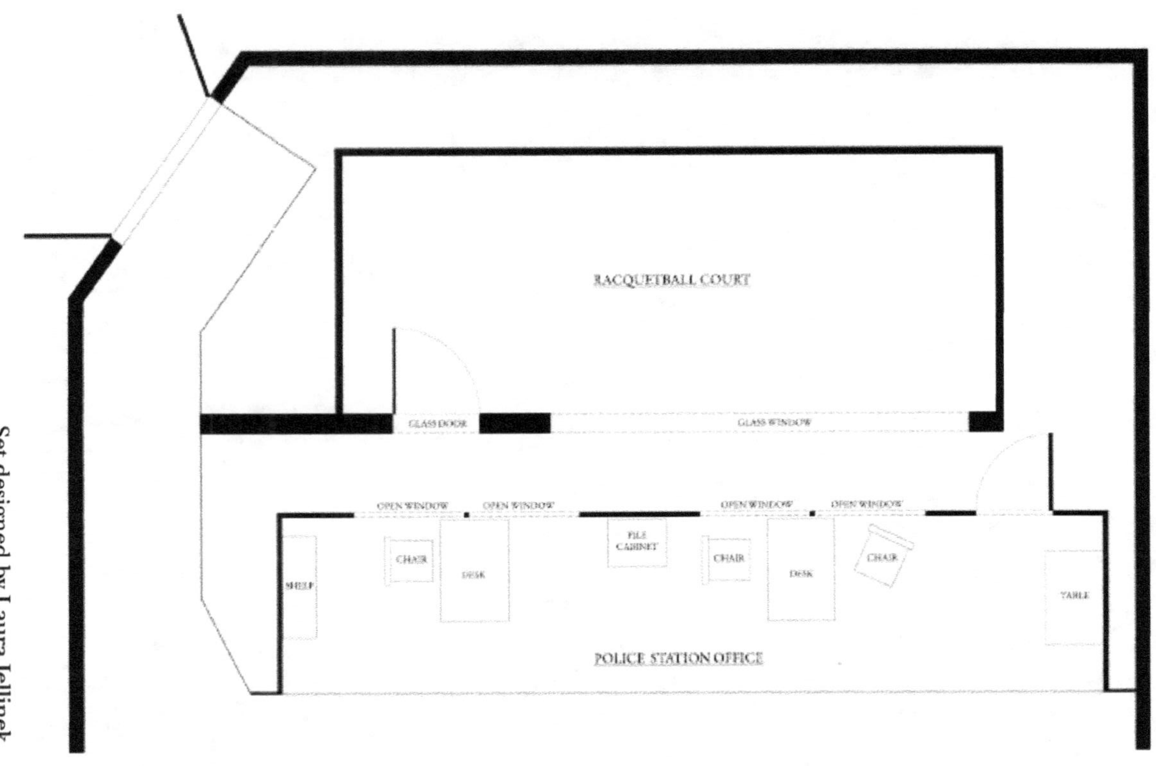

Set designed by Laura Jellinek

www.ingramcontent.com/pod-product-compliance
Lightning Source LLC
Chambersburg PA
CBHW070419120726
47909CB00005B/1716